She didn't want him to go.

The desire she felt was as clear as the sky on a bright, sunny day. There was neither confusion nor uncertainty. There was only the feeling she was exactly where she was meant to be, with the person she was meant to be with.

His arms, wonderfully warm through her damp clothes, went around her as he started to kiss her back, slowly at first, then with more urgency.

In that moment, she realized what she had known, in the deepest and darkest corner of her heart, all along.

It has always been him.

Kissing alone wouldn't satisfy her. She had never been more certain of something, ever. Her hands took a life of their own, moving beneath his shirt, until she could feel the hardness of his torso under her fingertips.

He didn't keep idle. He nipped at her earlobes and neck as he began to push the straps of the black dress off her shoulders, baring a wider path for his lips to trace.

She found her voice and, for what seemed like the very first time, the words to tell him what she truly wanted.

"Please don't go. Don't leave me tonight."

SHIRLEY SIATON

HEART CHAINED

A LOVE THEY COULD NEVER OUTRUN.

A NOVELLA

HEART CHAINED

A Novella

Copyright © 2024 Shirley Siaton Parabia

ALL RIGHTS RESERVED.

No part of this book may be reproduced or used in any manner without the prior written permission of the copyright owner, except for the use of brief quotations in a book review. To request permission, contact the publisher at books@inkysword.com.

This is a work of fiction. Names, characters, businesses, events and incidents are the products of the author's imagination. Any resemblance to actual persons, living or dead, or actual events is purely coincidental.

All brand and product names used in this book are trademarks, registered trademarks, or trade names of their respective owners. Inky Sword Book Publishing is not associated with any product or vendor in this book.

ISBN 978-6-21-837498-0 (pbk)

First Edition, January 2024

Published by Shirley S. Parabia

Inky Sword Book Publishing
Barangay Quezon, Arevalo, Iloilo City 5000
Republic of the Philippines
inkysword.com

Content Warnings

Warnings for explicit content, profanity, and references to violence.

Recommended for mature readers 18 years old and above.

Playlist

"Bring Me to Life"
Evanescence

"Everything"
Alanis Morissette

"One Last Breath"
Creed

"Into Your Arms"
Witt Lowry & Ava Max

"Here Without You"
3 Doors Down

"Gravity"
Sara Bareilles

"Stay"
Cueshe

To those who are done running, too.

TABLE OF CONTENTS

| ONE | Trina | The Return | 5 |
ONE	Trina	The Return	5
TWO	Vincent	The Secret	11
THREE	Trina	The Rain	25
FOUR	Vincent	The Race	29
FIVE	Trina	The Stranger	37
SIX	Vincent	The Turn	49
SEVEN	Trina	The Heart	57
EIGHT	Vincent	The Chains	65
NINE	Trina	The Touch	71
TEN	Vincent	The Light	77

About the Author	81
On the Web	83

Acknowledgments

I am very grateful to *MOD Filipina Magazine,* which gave a chance to my short story, *'Storms,'* the inspiration for this work, to be read the world over.

My gratitude to Harbinger Design for the gorgeous book cover and Dawn Black for formatting this manuscript beautifully.

A LOVE THEY COULD NEVER OUTRUN.

A NOVELLA

ONE
TRINA
THE RETURN

He was predictable, and she liked it that way. With Vincent Tugade, she always knew where she stood, what to expect. Everything about him was practically routine.

That morning, she immediately knew, the moment she saw a small box of cookies on her desk, that he was back. He had spent most of the past two months working offsite in Pampanga, in rounds of audits to wrap up the tax year. Although he wasn't the only auditor who had traveled there, she knew he was the only one who would remember to get her a gift, usually a sampling of the local delicacies.

Katrina David smiled and, delightedly, made her way across the building floor, from Human Resources to the side of the external auditors, which everyone in their firm called Assassins' Block.

Vincent's office was at a far corner, smaller than most but with an expansive view of Pasay City. The walls were almost bare except for a few framed certificates and photographs. It was always scented with the strong black coffee he drank all the time.

He was seated behind his two computer screens when she walked in. He looked up when he saw her. He jumped to his feet and swooped down on her for a hug.

"Welcome back, VAT," she said, putting her arms around him.

Years ago, when he first joined the firm, she had found his initials to be a little too fitting for his profession. As a result, she began using it. Then it stuck.

His familiar warmth was always comforting, as was the cool, subtle scent of his cologne.

"You look so brown. Eaten one too many plates of *sisig*?"

He laughed as he kissed her on the check. "Jealous much? It's good to be back. How have you been, Trina?"

"It's been busy around here," she said, giving him a peck in return. "I had no one to complain to these past few months, though. You missed a lot."

Vincent Alcon Tugade was the poster boy for yuppie Manila. He had classic Filipino looks, from his brown skin to his proud face with the hard planes, broad nose and dark eyes. He always dressed simply and elegantly, in light shirts and dark slacks, with hair neatly combed back. He appeared trustworthy and competent, without being obnoxious about any of it.

"I'm sure I did," he said. "With you around, I'll catch up in no time."

She sat on one of the chairs in front of his desk, one leg folded under her, and leaned forward. "How are you? Did anything exciting happen in Pampanga?"

"If you call spending fourteen hours a day with ledgers exciting, by all means, it was very exciting. I had the time of my life."

"You're no fun, Vince."

"You're welcome to all the fun, Trina." His smile at her was nothing if not indulgent, like a patient adult to a restless child. "I'll stick to my balance sheets. I don't think I've got energy for much else."

She frowned at him, exasperated but unsurprised. If he wasn't Vincent, she would have felt patronized. They were about the same age, but she had long since accepted that he behaved like a much older man. Her own father, who was into Airsoft and war games tournaments, was more fun than him.

She pouted at him. "Well, you'd better have enough energy to dance at my wedding, at least."

His hand froze over the computer mouse, just as one of his eyebrows shot up into his hairline. It took a second before he said anything.

"Abella asked?"

"He's going to." Trina saw he was about to say something more, but she stopped him by interrupting. "Soon. Maybe this weekend. We're having dinner on Saturday night. He's pulling out all the stops, VAT. Five-star hotel, the works."

She watched him lean back in his chair.

Broad-shouldered, well spoken, neat, and fairly easy to fit in the bill of tall, dark and handsome, he would have been very cute, she thought objectively, had he not been so boring.

Mature, she corrected herself, loyally. *He's just mature.*

"Well, in exchange for the cookies, I'm claiming first dibs on the happy news."

Trina stood up and rolled her eyes. She would have liked to stay if not for their department's Monday morning meeting.

"I've got to go for our team meeting. I never knew those cookies had a price, though."

"Miss David, you have worked for this firm your entire professional life." He switched to what she called his Presentation Mode, which he usually assumed in meetings with clients. It was the most deathly serious and, somehow, also one of the most comical voices she'd ever heard. "You should know by now that everything has a price."

Maybe he wasn't so boring, after all.

Two
Vincent

The Secret

It was Saturday.

He picked up a dart from the coffee table in the middle of his apartment, aimed, and took the shot. The dart found its target, a small square of paper he had tacked to his reminders board.

Vincent walked up to the board and removed the dart. It had pierced right through the piece of desk calendar for that month, exactly where he had intended it to.

Today. *Saturday.*

He woke up that morning the same time he did every day, at five sharp. His apartment was close to Pasay City Sports Complex, so on most days he would go for a run. Today was no different.

After his run, he returned to his place and cooked oatmeal and eggs for breakfast. If he was not working weekends or on travel somewhere, he preferred staying in. If he had the chance, he would go out on Friday and Saturday nights.

Tonight, he definitely was going out. He needed to get out.

He had received the announcement the night before, at eleven, by text message.

R1: 100% Stock Engine & Chassis
R2: Stock 4Stroke
R3: Stock 4Stroke Automatic
R4: Open to All Brands & Models
Track: Legal confirm 8PM Sat 22/4
Entry: TBC msg 9PM Sat 22/4

Vincent Tugade was a drag racer in the Manila underground circuit. His moniker, for many years now, was the King of Chains, from the insignia on the hood of his glistening black Dodge, paired with his signature leather clothing of the same color. His father had sketched this design for a race car back in the day; he had taken it upon himself to bring it to life.

He was into cars as far back as he could remember, spending long hours with his father at their garage during weekends, learning as much as he could about automobile design and engines.

Although his father had been a government tax official, his passion was customizing cars, which he had passed on to his son.

Vincent had been racing since he was eighteen, two years after his parents died from a freak traffic accident that involved a drunk driver ramming his pick-up truck into their own car. It was a bitter, ugly kind of irony.

He had uprooted himself and his little sister Veronica, ten years old at the time, from their province, and came to Metro Manila to live with one of their aunts, who taught at a Catholic private school. He had worked at the school as an errand boy at first, which led to the discovery of his near-prodigious understanding of numbers when he balanced the books of the school cafeteria and the uniform shop in less than a week.

Around the time, one of his jobs at his aunt's house was to look after her car, an ancient orange Toyota with manual transmission. He had been searching for a replacement for the stick shift at one of the shops in Makati when he overheard two men discussing an upcoming 'race.' That had piqued his curiosity in no time. Not long after, he had secretly souped up his aunt's

ToyoPet and brought it for a run at an open race one night in late summer, just before he was due to start college.

By the time he graduated and got an Accountancy degree, he had garnered enough supporters and winnings to get his own car. An auditor's job allowed him more financial freedom to support his sister through university, buy a second car, and lease-to-own the condominium he now lived in.

Two years ago, his aunt had passed away quietly from a long-term illness. His little sister, after years of looking after their aunt, had decided to put her Nursing degree to good use and returned to their home province to take a high-profile clinical instructor job.

The glorious bachelor life allowed him to work as much as he liked with numbers during the day and race as much as he wanted at night. It was a simple delineation of the things he was good at.

He was on his second cup of coffee and was about to go downstairs to the parking basement to check his car for the night's race when his phone rang.

The name on the screen was the least expected of all. The presence of Katrina David was the only fluctuating value in the perfectly balanced books of his work and personal life.

He picked up the call.

"Hello, Trina." He tried to keep his voice as neutral as possible. "How are you?"

To his surprise, the response at the other end of the line was not the usual exuberant one he was familiar with. "Hi, Vince. I'm so sorry for bothering you. Did I call at a bad time?"

It was Trina, but she sounded so subdued it was like he was talking to an entirely different person.

"No, not at all. Everything okay?"

"You got a minute to talk? Please?"

No nicknames, no jokes, no comments on the absence of fun in his life. Maybe he had somehow wandered into a more depressing alternate reality after his early-morning run.

"Sure, of course. Anything for you." He took a seat on his couch. "What's up?"

"Nothing." There was a long, strained pause from her. "I mean, not nothing, but it's something I can't talk about with my parents or my friends."

"I'm all ears. What's this about?"

"James."

"Abella?"

The prick?

He wanted to tack on his opinion, but decided to keep his mouth shut.

The thought of James Abella, Trina's boyfriend, gave him the sudden urge to punch something. Vincent disliked him the same way he disliked racers who would rather spend money on a custom paint job than change their engine oil after a few races.

He had only met Abella three times at office functions over the past year or so but had long since formed the impression that the man was all flash, no substance. Perhaps a career in modeling did that to a person, but Vincent never generalized and only gave informed opinions. Since Trina was not a client, he kept whatever sentiments he had to himself.

"Has he done something? Are you okay?"

"Nothing like that. I'm fine."

He tried to be patient, thinking of the way he would usually talk to his little sister when she opened up about her relationships. "Okay, then, Trina. Just let me know if there's anything I can do."

Maybe, just maybe, run Abella over. She could pick which car I should use.

"Vince...what happens if I don't want to?"

"Don't want to what?"

"You know. The S-word."

He almost sputtered on his coffee. He slowly put his mug down on the table to avoid any further incident.

Damn. So much for your regular Saturday morning routine.

He held the phone away from his mouth as he took a deep breath before responding.

"I thought everything was done, dusted and double-ruled, all that. He was going to ask you to marry him, wasn't he?"

"He wants to take our relationship further, has wanted to for a while now. If he does ask me tonight to marry him and I say yes, he might want a..."

"Test drive?" He completed the statement and immediately regretted it.

"Yes." Deadpan and humorless, Trina had probably been replaced by an alien who happened to mimic her voice very well.

The silence on the line stretched for what seemed like hours.

There was only one response he could utter, the only one that mattered.

"What do you want to do?"

He heard a huge intake of breath, before she continued in a shaky voice. "I don't know. That's why I called you, to ask a man how he would feel if his fiancée refused to…you know."

This was dangerous ground. He would never speak for the prick.

"Has he asked you before?" He swallowed very hard before continuing. "Have you done it with him before?"

Fuck.

He could feel it. His face was going red. He was supposed to give advice on depreciation and inventory, not sex and relationships.

"No. Never. I tried, Vince. I can't…" Trina's voice trailed off.

He was tempted to ask why, but it wasn't the gentlemanly thing to do. If there was one thing he knew about women, it was to give them space.

As Trina went on, she sounded more and more anxious with each word. "He hasn't asked me straight out. But what he does when we're alone, it's enough to tell me what he really wants. I know I'm supposed to like it. He's my boyfriend, after all. But I can't seem to get myself to give in."

He listened to her breathing for several long moments before he spoke, as gently and as patiently as he could. "Then don't give in, if you don't want to."

"Wouldn't that frustrate him, or make him angry? Turn him off?"

Vincent knew about frustration very well, but this was not about him. "If he really loves you and wants to marry you, he should damn well be willing to wait until you're ready."

"Would you wait, Vince?" Her voice was quiet. "If you were in his place?"

"You know me better than that. I would never even consider putting you in a predicament like this. That's not love, Trina. Not even close."

Damn it to hell.

This wasn't supposed to be about him. Not in the fucking least.

"I never thought of it that way," she said. "When James first became my boyfriend, I was so happy. Everyone kept telling me how lucky I was."

Not everyone, he wanted to correct her.

"He is so handsome and dreamy, you know? He is a famous model and all that. I thought I have to keep him happy, to keep him."

"Are you happy now?" That seemed to be the last word he could think of to describe her at the moment.

"To be honest, it's hard to be happy when your relationship is like a ticking time bomb. Lately, all I could think about is that it's only a matter of time before James asks. What if I can't give him what he wants? What if I make the wrong decision? What if he leaves me?"

It didn't sound like a healthy relationship. It sounded an awful lot like co-dependency.

"What if you think about what would make you happy, Trina?"

"Me? I don't know."

He couldn't blame her. Sometimes being in the safety of one's comfort zone mattered more than pursuing happiness. Sometimes the risk of getting out wasn't worth it, if it meant venturing into the unknown.

If it meant getting hurt.

"Once you figure it out, I get first dibs. I'll be here to listen. I might even splurge on some cookies. You know, those nasty sweet ones from Greenbelt you like so much."

He was rewarded by a small giggle. "Yeah, those."

"Think about what would make you happy, Trina, and make your decisions based on that. Not on what would make someone else happy, especially at your expense."

He hoped there was at least some clarity in her mind, or even a hint of a smile on her face.

"Thanks, VAT," she finally said. "You're the best, you know that?"

"Don't tell anyone, okay? My services are exclusive."

"To me?" He could hear the coyness, the humor, back in her voice. It was the best he could ask for, under the circumstances.

"Always have been."

"See you Monday, Vince. I'm really sorry if I bothered you on your weekend."

"It's okay. You can bother me anytime."

Trina thanked him again and hung up.

He stood up, plugged the phone into its charger, and sat back down on the couch. He picked up his mug for a sip. The coffee was now cold and flat, almost bitter.

He felt just as cold and flat as he thought of Abella, with her.

Trina.

He first met her six years ago, when she did his pre-interview at the firm. She was the most breathtaking woman he had ever laid eyes on, an opinion the years had not changed. She had smooth caramel skin, an hourglass figure, and long wavy hair a deep shade of mahogany.

Her face had a sincere warmth he could just stare at and drink in for hours.

His first impression was that she was the human equivalent of the Energizer bunny, someone who kept going and going and barely stopped talking while at it.

Instead of finding her lively manner annoying, he found himself warming up, to the point of allowing her to christen him with a new nickname. It was little wonder she was the one usually assigned to potential hires or new employees.

It was a wonder, however, how they became friends. The first thing he could think of was how she could so easily get him to open up, or at least talk. Other people at the firm, even his fellow auditors, gave him space to work and move around the office without much need for social interaction. He had a reputation for no-frills efficiency, and he had to admit it commanded respect.

Trina did not give him the wide berth others did. She simply found her way into his life and settled in it, the same way she would barge into his office any time she wanted and sit in weird positions on the chairs facing his desk. Their friendship had lasted the better part of the past five years, to the point that his sister thought she was his girlfriend when Trina showed up at their aunt's funeral.

Now, he pondered the advice he had given her.

Think about what would make you happy.

Was he a hypocrite to give a confused woman this kind of advice, when he couldn't even apply it to his own life?

Then again, he wasn't the one in a relationship, not the one who faced the risk of a broken heart.

Or was he?

He knew from the moment Trina had started talking about things getting serious with Abella that his own heart was on the line. It was only a matter of time before it got ripped into shreds. He predicted it would either be at the sight of a ring on her finger or of the very woman herself in a wedding dress.

He was prepared for it, as long as she didn't know. He could face it, the same way he had faced life when it came to her.

Held back by chains of his own making.

Three
Trina

The Rain

Done, *dusted and double ruled.*

Vincent's words echoed in her mind as she lifted her chin and walked straight into the drizzling Manila night, ignoring the politely disguised yet obviously curious stares of the doorman and security guard stationed at the hotel's front entrance.

More like fully depreciated and written off.

She was a fool to think there would be at least some sort of compromise, that James would give her room to think about what she really wanted.

Instead, he had wined and dined her, then went in for the kill.

It shouldn't have surprised her.

The rain was the first one that month, adding insult to her already dreary state of affairs. The typhoon season was still months away, but, hell, anything goes.

Life seemed to be trying to throw as much crap as it could at her, all at the same time.

The hotel was located in the Bay Area, close to the metropolitan but posh and exclusive enough to merit its high profile and ludicrously expensive status.

There should be a few taxis around, in theory, but everyone drove their shiny, showy cars to and from this place, as far as she could see.

She was the only one walking.

She could wait inside for a taxi, but she had more pride than that. No way in hell was she staying.

Trina clutched her leather handbag tightly, debating whether or not to use it as some kind of umbrella, finally dismissing the idea as pointless.

Her little black dress and matching suede shoes had already gone to waste. She wished she had not splurged as much during her shopping trip that afternoon, in an effort to keep her mind off the conversation with Vincent and the inevitable with James.

The downpour had increased in intensity by the time she reached the main gates of the hotel. Half-blinded by rain water, she continued to plod onwards.

"I met someone else, Trina."

Those five words tolled at the back of her head like some kind of death knell.

James had gone on and on with his explanation. Perhaps he'd thought it would make her feel better, if there was a clear reason for their break-up.

"I thought you loved me, but I never felt it. She made me feel loved, in ways more than words could ever explain."

Feel it, my ass, she thought bitterly.

"I tried to make our relationship work but nothing ever seemed to get through to you. I hope you'll understand where I'm coming from. I've fallen in love with her."

The funny part was that she understood very clearly, maybe a little too well for her own good.

The moment her now-ex-boyfriend had finished his confession, she had stood up, with as much dignity as she could muster, and made the most regal exit she could from the restaurant.

She took pride in two things: First, she'd kept her head held high; second, she'd never cried.

She had no desire to cry. If anything, she could almost describe her feelings, after the initial hurtful blow of rejection to her ego, as a combination of relief and lightness, as if she'd just been unburdened of something ridiculously heavy.

"Think about what would make you happy, Trina."

She would give anything right now, if she could just talk to Vincent.

Anything to hear his voice, always a source of comfort and reason.

As soon as she got home, she'd try and give him a call…

A sudden, deafening screech cut through the fog of her thoughts.

She momentarily forgot her troubles as she, dazed and confused, faced the direction of the high-pitched sound.

A black car, with prism-like headlights, had stopped a few feet away from her. She stared as the car's wipers moved furiously, rhythmically, across the windshield.

She had not seen any cars coming her way. There was no one else outside, no one else on the road. Not in this weather.

She was meant to be on her own tonight, wasn't she? Chained to her own thoughts and, even more so, her regrets.

But it wasn't meant to be.

FOUR
VINCENT

THE RACE

It was time.

Even after all these years, anticipation gripped him at the thought of a race.

The feeling was familiar: the slight acceleration of his heartbeat, the clammy sensation in his palms, the tightness in his stomach. Soon enough, nerves would give way to focus; and focus would eventually explode into all-consuming adrenaline once the flag came down.

In the dimly lit garage of his apartment building, the sleek form of his car, whom he'd named *Eskeleto*, stood before him, ready to carry him into yet another race.

He inspected every inch of the vehicle, ensuring its peak performance. He let his hands run over the smooth curves of the car, grounding himself in the present, as far as he possibly could from thoughts that threatened to invade his impeccably crafted sense of concentration.

Right now, he hated the accuracy and precision of his memory. Because of it, there were images of Trina floating at the fringes of his mind, clawing at the walls he had so carefully built to keep his emotions in check.

"Let's do this, old friend," he said to *Eskeleto*.

Just like the well-worn leather jacket he had on, the car's hood bore his insignia of a skull encircled by a chain and an antique pocket watch.

It was as fearsome a symbol as it was poetic; a juxtaposition of life, death, and the confines of mortality.

Time.

What he wouldn't give to have more time with Trina, before she went on with her life and rode off into the sunset with her male model.

He sighed.

He really was fucked.

He had no choice now but to deal with it head on, all cylinders firing.

He had to deal with the thought of losing Trina.

As the King of Chains of the Manila drag race circuit, he had one glaring solution to his current predicament: *Drive.*

Vincent slipped behind the wheel and switched the ignition, his hands settling comfortably on the steering wheel.

Next to *Eskeleto* stood his other car, the dark grey Toyota sedan he used to drive to work and other more everyday places. He'd named the car *T-Baby*.

Thinking about himself doing something so juvenile and lovesick was almost painful.

At least, *T-Baby* was there to stay.

As *Eskeleto* roared to life beneath him, he allowed the sound to drown out all else. With one last glance at his other car, as if bidding farewell to a part of him that still clung to the possibility of going in another direction, towards a different destination, he revved the engine and sped off into the night.

The city lights blurred together as he drove through the streets. He knew each race demanded every ounce of skill, focus and determination he could muster. He couldn't afford to give in to sentimentality or distractions.

He made it to the venue with time to spare. Situated next to Manila Bay, the track was abuzz with the frenetic energy of the underground scene, where the salty breeze coming in from the sea mingled with the scents of rubber and gasoline. The sounds of engines revving and people shouting greetings and good-natured taunts to each other were comforting to his ears, a welcome diversion from his inner turmoil.

He parked in his designated spot near the track, the area marked by a replica of his skull symbol using temporary neon paint. He took a deep breath and stepped out of the car to check in with the organizers of the evening's race.

"King of Chains!" a voice called out.

A group of younger racers, clustered along with their brightly colored sports cars, looked at him with awe and reverence.

"H-hey, boss," one of them stammered, extending a trembling hand. "Good luck tonight!"

"Thanks," Vincent replied, forcing a smile for their benefit. "Good luck to all of you. Let's have a good race tonight."

As he shook hands with well-wishers, he allowed himself to slip into his track persona: someone confident, untouchable, and utterly devoted to the thrill of the race.

"Vincent! Over here!" a chorus of female voices beckoned him from a nearby cluster of cars.

He turned to see a gaggle of beautiful women, some draped over sleek hoods and others leaning against gleaming fenders. A few cast sultry glances his way.

"Looking good tonight, Vincent," purred one woman whose perfectly made-up face he'd seen at almost every race for the past few years.

Her name was Alena; she drove a custom red Volvo that he was quite sure was also bulletproof.

"How about we celebrate your victory together later?" Her voice was heavily laced with suggestive promise.

"Sorry, beautiful, not tonight," he replied with a polite smile. "Got to travel for work tomorrow."

Though his reputation on the track often attracted such propositions, tonight his heart and mind were too preoccupied to entertain even the fleeting distractions of flirtation and casual sex.

"Always so focused," another woman teased, boldly stepping closer to ruffle his hair. It was Florence, an oil tycoon's daughter, who drove an import Lamborghini that probably cost more than a lifetime's worth of his salary. "That's what makes you the best."

"I'll make it up to you next time, ladies," he promised with a grin, though the words felt hollow to his ears.

As he turned away from the women and eventually found his way to the organizers, the clamor of the race track seemed to amplify within his head.

He *needed* tonight's race, more than he'd ever needed any other race before.

Trina.

The name echoed through this head, almost forming on his lips like a prayer for salvation.

His prayer was answered not too long after, when he found himself flanked by two other cars on each side at the starting line.

His opponents were mere shadows in his peripheral vision, their presence barely registering as his hands settled on the wheel with the familiarity of a swordsman with his trusty katana.

"Are you ready?" came a woman's voice through a megaphone. "It's time for the final race!"

That night's honorary marshal was a beauty queen from a neighboring country. She was unbelievably attractive in person, with a glistening black bob, legs that went on for days, and a tiny waist cinched in by the matching belt of her red dress.

She held up a racing flag in the air, her movement punctuated by excited cheers and roars of the crowd.

"GO!"

In an instant, the world around him melted away, fading into streaks of color as his car shot forward like a bullet from a gun. Adrenaline surged through his veins as he expertly navigated the twists and turns of the track.

As he raced towards the finish line, the cheers of the crowd reverberated in his ears, but none quite reached him.

He knew what was missing, but he also knew he had to keep himself in check long enough to finish what he'd started. The final stretch lay before him, a straight path to victory.

And, just like that, it was over.

Vincent and *Eskeleto* crossed the finish line, the other racers and their cars still dozens of meters behind.

The moment he stepped out of the car, he was surrounded by a boisterous crowd. He lost count of the handshakes, hugs, and kisses he was given, but he took it all in stride.

Somehow, tonight, he didn't feel the usual rush of victory. The end of the race, albeit one he'd won, felt like signing off the financial statements of a client at the end of a lengthy audit.

It was a job he did well, a job he'd completed meticulously and painstakingly. No more, no less.

"Nice win, King of Chains," one of his opponents called out, clapping him on the shoulder.

"Thanks, Phil," he replied, forcing a smile.

As the last remnants of the crowd dispersed into after-parties and the track finally fell silent, Vincent climbed back into his car.

Just as he started the drive back to his apartment, opting for a shortcut through the Bay Area, it began to rain.

The streets of late-night Manila stretched out before him like a labyrinth, but he realized there was no escaping the thoughts that haunted him, no matter where he went.

He could drive fast, drive away, or even drive endlessly. These were all tempting options, but he knew, in the end, escape was impossible.

Vincent knew he could never outrun his thoughts of her, tightly chained to his memories and his heart.

He didn't even get that far when he saw her in the middle of the rain-slicked road. Shock mingling with disbelief, he dimly heard the tires screech as he hit the brakes.

Heart pounding, he stared at the drenched figure standing outside his car, illuminated by *Eskeleto*'s headlights.

It's not a mirage, he thought, his head spinning.

He would recognize the real Trina anywhere.

Was it a sign, or some kind of twisted joke?

There was only one way to find out.

He pushed the car door open and stepped out into the downpour.

FIVE
TRINA

THE STRANGER

A man, dressed all in the same color as the dark vehicle before her, stepped out of the car.

His clothing was shiny, like leather. With his hair styled into spikes, he looked like a sleek nocturnal animal, or maybe the lead singer of a rock band.

"Trina? What the fuck are you doing here?"

The voice was very familiar, but the sight wasn't. The rain and the headlights danced around her like strobes in a disco, making her dizzy.

She had to make sense of this.

So she uttered his name, in both uncertainty and unabashed curiosity.

"Vincent?"

The man who sounded but barely looked like Vincent Tugade sloshed his way to her side, his eyes glittering even in the cover of night.

"Have you lost your mind, Trina? You shouldn't be out on the road like this."

"Vincent?" she repeated the name, not quite sure if she wanted to be right or wrong. "What are you doing here? Why do you look like that?"

"We have to get you off the streets." He held out a hand to her. "Come on."

She could only stare at him. The dinner, the near-accident, now this man. It was too much.

"Get in the car, Trina, please."

She backed away. She didn't have the energy to put up with more surprises tonight. "Just go, okay? Leave me alone."

"What are you doing?" He stepped closer and took hold of her arm. "I'm taking you home, okay? Please get in the car and we can talk about it."

He gave her that familiar indulgent smile, none too sincerely this time. She recognized him like this, vaguely.

"I don't think—"

Before she could continue, he had his hand on the small of her back and was guiding her to the car. Too weary to put up a fight, she allowed herself to be pushed, albeit gently, into the front seat.

He silently got into the driver's side. In the dim light, she could see his lips set in a firm line. He took off his jacket and gave it to her. He was dressed in a black sleeveless shirt underneath.

"Stay warm. I'll turn off the air conditioner."

"Thanks," she heard herself say.

"You're welcome."

He reached for the dashboard and started adjusting buttons and switches. His arms had well-defined muscles and an assortment of tattoos going all the way down to his forearms.

To stop herself from staring at him so rudely, Trina gave the jacket a shake and put it around her shoulders. She could feel her new dress soak water into the car seat. She buckled up when she saw him do the same. She clutched her bag and the seatbelt close to her as she looked out of the window at the rainy night.

The car hummed to life and started to cruise forward.

"Vince, I..." It took a while before she could work up the energy and courage to look at the almost-stranger next to her, much less talk to him.

"I'm sorry," she completed lamely, clenching her hands, feeling them shake with the residual cold.

He was quiet for several seconds. "For what?"

"For all the trouble. One thing after another went downhill. Before I knew it, I was out of there like my ass was on fire."

He shook his head, but kept his eyes trained on the road. "In a way, it's a good thing I was the one you ran into. The car's brakes hold up pretty well even when they're wet."

The thought of brakes was enough to make her feel even colder. Had it been another car, or another driver, she wasn't quite sure where she would be now.

In hindsight, she should have stayed inside the hotel and waited for a taxi, or got James to drop her home, not wandered out into the rain like some tragic heroine in a cheap romance novel. The only real tragedy of the entire evening was the sorry shape of her pricey new dress and its matching shoes.

"Still, this entire drama is my fault," she admitted.

"Drama?"

"The walk-out, the emoting in the rain, the getting nearly ran over part. I guess I was too proud to put up with any more bullshit."

"I see." Vincent held on to the steering wheel with one hand, his other hand going up to rub out droplets of water stuck to his spiky hair. "I'm sure that wasn't how you had the night planned out, was it?"

"Well, no." She gave her eyes a little rub, still unable to reconcile the fact that this tattooed, leather-clad man was the Vincent she had known all these years. She didn't even know he had arms like that.

For the first time, she noted that this wasn't his Toyota sedan, but something else entirely.

The black car had metal panels on the sides, a convex roof and a windshield lined with what looked like steel reinforcements. The seats were wrapped in dark leather that matched his clothes. All over the interior, there were stickers and buttons with death motifs, such as skulls, chains and spikes. The buttons and gauges on the dashboard before her looked like the control panel of a mad scientist.

His voice was calm and measured as he spoke. "If I had known you were going to be at the hotel, I would have picked you up. You should have called me."

"I dragged you through the pathetic story of my relationship this morning. I could never do that to you twice. Besides, I never thought you would be here, at this time. Like that." She gestured to all of him in general.

"Like what?" He glanced at her, tilting his head curiously.

"Like, different. Dangerous. You know, someone capable of running James over."

To her surprise, he smiled. "Whoever said I wasn't? All you have to do is ask."

She sighed. "That sounds very tempting right now."

His next words were so serious it was hard to discern whether or not he really meant them. "If you really want to do a number on Abella, we can turn back and get him. The track near the bay will be closed by now, but I'm sure I could get us in. I've raced there since they started building it, right after the mall opened."

Race.

VAT was a racer. Suddenly, the car, the clothes and the skulls all made sense.

"Thanks for the generous and potentially criminal offer, but I'll pass." She could feel the beginnings of a small smile on her lips.

They didn't talk for a while as he deftly wove the car through the Saturday night traffic of the city, taking shortcuts through tiny side streets. By the time they were out of the Bay Area, she felt calm enough to loosen her grip on her bag and the seatbelt and settle more comfortably in the front seat.

"You still live at the tower?"

"Yes. I'm surprised you remember."

He shrugged. "We should be there soon. I know a shortcut near the hospital. That should keep us away from most of the late night traffic."

"You're the best, VAT," she said, echoing her sentiments from earlier that day. "Thanks for putting up with my crap."

He didn't answer, but a little while later she felt his hand on her shoulder.

"It's not crap. I'm very sorry this happened." He gave a gentle squeeze before letting go. "You deserve to be happy."

She tugged at his jacket, pulling it more snugly around her. She never knew leather could feel so soft.

"At least James had the guts to call it off himself. I suppose he needed something I couldn't give. We both wanted different things. I stressed all about it for nothing."

Vincent shook his head. "Not nothing. I'm sure whatever you two had, it meant more to you than it did to him."

Trina looked out the window again. She could barely see a thing, except for torrents of water, thick mist, and flickering lights.

It was a fitting metaphor for what she had with James. What she thought she had with him. She never really saw what it was, just blurry lines and splashes of color. Everything she made out of it was her own interpretation, not the truth.

Her newly-ended relationship was a joke, if not a failure, from the very start. Marrying her was something James had never even remotely considered. She knew that now.

"James told me he met someone else while on a job in Bali months back. It doesn't take a genius to figure out he got what he wanted from her. Apparently they kept in touch after that."

The memory of her ex's confession was still fresh in her mind, spilling out easily. Trina couldn't even remember the other girl's name. "James said she was far less…I don't know, frigid than I am, I suppose. The exact words he used were 'cold' and 'walled off.'"

"Sounds like he thinks you're some kind of high security vault. One he doesn't have the access code to, the poor bastard."

"I never thought you'd ever feel sorry for him." She gave him a sidelong glance. "You hate his guts."

"Am I that obvious?"

"Kind of, especially as you offered to run him over if I wanted you to."

"That prick doesn't know what he's missing out on," he declared solemnly, in a tone that begged no argument.

Minutes later, they pulled up in front of a high-rise condominium complex. He parked in an open spot on the sidewalk, got out of the car, and opened the passenger door for her.

She shakily stepped out, her wet shoes digging into her skin as she walked carefully on the rain-drenched pavement. Her dress had dried partially, but it still clung to her body like a second skin. To her surprise, she felt self-conscious under the bright fluorescent lights of the building's main entrance as he followed her to the foyer.

"Thank you, Vince." She pulled his jacket off her shoulders and handed it back to him. "For everything."

"You're welcome." He reached out and took the jacket back. "Will you be okay? Can I get you anything, from the pharmacy or somewhere?"

"No, I'm fine. Thanks for the offer." No matter how he dressed, he was always reliable.

Tonight, he just appeared a little more exciting than usual.

It occurred to her how different it had felt to look at her ex-boyfriend's mestizo, camera-ready face, compared to the darker, harder countenance of the man before her.

With Vincent, she had always been at ease. She never had to second-guess herself or question her own actions and decisions.

His words in the car rattled around the back of her mind.

That prick doesn't know what he's missing out on.

What if she asked herself that question?

What am I missing out on?

He was looking straight back at her. She had no idea what was in his head. She never really had. She'd always expected him, by default, to come through, listen, accept, and give – cookies, advice, time, his presence. He even came through for her at this time, without her asking, without him knowing, by sheer chance of fate.

Why did he?

Trina didn't know if she felt guilty, confused or overwhelmed. Perhaps all three. Seeing Vincent in a different light, in the rainy cold of reality, was unnerving.

She needed to put this entire weekend behind her, as soon as possible.

He stepped closer and wrapped one arm around her shoulders. He gave her a quick peck on the cheek; it felt familiar, yet, in her waterlogged state, she felt a little breathless at the contact. She could feel blood rushing to her head.

"Rest up, Trina," he said as he pulled away. "Call me tomorrow if you need anything, okay?"

She didn't let him pull away completely. Instead, she put her hands on his tattooed forearms. Still halfway in his embrace, she could see that his eyes were almost silver in color, not the greyish-brown she thought they were.

"Would you like to come up for some coffee?" Her own voice sounded higher-pitched, even shrill, to her own ears. She had no idea where it came from, but it was all her.

He hesitated. He was still predictable enough, but she had always liked that about him. She knew his answer before he said it, but she didn't quite anticipate the tension she felt emanating from his body.

"Sure."

SIX
VINCENT

THE TURN

What the fuck are you doing, Tugade?

Vincent mentally confronted himself as he followed her off the elevator. They had reached the seventh floor of her apartment building.

"My place is this way." Trina was a few steps ahead. He could see she was limping a little and dragging her feet. He thought of helping her, but the idea of touching her again didn't sound very smart at the moment.

He shouldn't have touched her like he had downstairs. They had always hugged and kissed each other chastely, but, tonight, it felt very different. For starters, she kept giving him wide-eyed looks, from all directions, as if she was seeing him for the first time.

Vince knew those kinds of looks. He had given her those before, many times over, when he was certain she couldn't see him. He had never stopped, not since he first saw her when she came out to the firm's lobby for his pre-interview.

He knew his feelings for her very well, had grappled with and successfully kept them buried under a platonic veneer. Trina, on the other, had no idea. If she did, she would probably be out of his life like her 'ass was on fire.'

It was a risk he could not take. He had too much to lose. Her friendship, her trust, and, above all, *her.*

Katrina David was someone he could never afford to lose.

With her freshly single from a break-up, this was the worst possible time to even consider that he had a chance. He would rather have himself run over on the track by the other racers.

Trina stopped at a unit numbered 704. "Home sweet home. Can you help me, Vince?"

He had to snap himself out of any delusional episode he had going. She was holding out her keys.

"The gold one, please."

He took the bunch rather abruptly from her grasp and moved closer to the door. As he bent over to unlock it, he felt Trina wrap her arms around his left arm as she leaned against him. Up close, he could see her wet dress hugging every curve of her body. Her cleavage was practically next to his face as she shifted her weight from foot to foot.

"I'm so tired, Vince," she said. "I think I spent next month's salary shopping this afternoon for an outfit that I completely ruined."

Ruined? That was the last thing on his mind, looking at her in the little black dress.

He averted his eyes and thanked all existing higher powers when he heard the lock give way. He was too close for comfort. He would have that coffee and get himself the fuck home.

She did not let him go as they went in, clinging to his arm as she hobbled into the apartment and pointed out the light switches. He gave in to his earlier gentlemanly inclination and led her to the white couch in the middle of her living room. She heaved herself gratefully onto the seat and took off her shoes.

"Major ouch." She shook her head and made clucking sounds as she started flexing her toes and rotating her ankles.

He took the opportunity to step away from her. He could leave. She was fine. He had made sure of that.

"I think I'll call it a night," he said. "I'd better go."

True to form, Trina hopped back to her bare feet. "What are you talking about? Sit down. Let me get you that coffee. It's premium roasted Arabica. I'll even give you the rest of the beans, too."

He swallowed hard and seated himself hesitantly on the couch, next to the spot she had just vacated. He tossed his jacket to a nearby plastic chair. "I'm sorry about the wet clothes."

"I did the same thing to your car. Call it even between us."

He watched her disappear behind a curtained doorway. He looked around. The place was neat and orderly; the colors were a mishmash of white, brown, orange and yellow. Even on a rainy night, the place looked bright and alive.

Minutes later, he saw her head poke through the curtains. "Vince? Come join me in the kitchen. I put on some croissants, too."

"That would be great." He stood up and followed her into the next room. It was fairly compact, cozy, outfitted with sunny yellow tiles. Next to a small glass window overlooking the city, there was a wooden table with matching seats for three.

She gestured for him to sit on one of the chairs. She was quiet as she poured them both coffee. She placed a plate full of croissants between them and sat from across him.

"Thanks for looking out for me tonight. Goodness knows I have no business troubling you for anything. I honestly thought this morning was the end of it."

He took a sip of the coffee. It was strong and scalding hot. "Is that how you think of yourself, Trina? Trouble?"

He watched her take a sip of coffee, twitching a little uncomfortably in her damp dress as she thought about his question. He wondered if it would be appropriate if he suggested she change clothes, more for his state of mind than her own health and comfort.

"It seems I could never give anyone what they want from me," she declared thoughtfully. "I don't know if that's trouble or not."

"It's called making your choices, I believe. Definitely not trouble."

Trina shrugged. "Is it? James thinks I'm a cold bitch. My friends think I'm so flighty I couldn't even commit to their vacation plans. My own family thinks I'm all talk and no substance, that's why I haven't been promoted to HR Manager."

The rapid-fire honesty in her declaration was a heart-rending surprise. He was sorely tempted to close the distance between them and take her into his arms.

Instead, he took another sip of coffee. "Do you agree with any of them?"

She shook her head. "I love my job and I like people. I actually enjoy my work. If I were manager, I would have to spend the whole damn day writing reports, signing stupid forms, and talking to higher management. As for trips, I don't really want to go on a lot of them because traveling's so expensive and I want to pay off this unit as soon as possible."

Her down-to-earth practicality was something he admired immensely. "Can't argue with the numbers on that one."

"I know, right?" Her shoulders heaved in a sigh. "And James…well, tonight pretty much sums it all up. For the record, he broke it off, but I was the one who walked out first."

"There you go. You've made your choices. If people don't appreciate that, it's their problem, not yours."

She smiled at him for what seemed the first time that evening. "I think you're right."

"You should start thinking about what you want, rather than what other people want and expect from you. As I said, you deserve to be happy. Do what makes you happy."

If only he could do the same thing. If only he had the balls to follow his own advice.

Her smile brightened a little more. "This makes me happy. Having you here."

It felt as if she had stabbed him, front and center. To disguise the tightness in his chest, he affected a grin and lifted his coffee mug in a toast. "To your happiness, Trina."

She leaned forward, wrapping her hands around her mug. Her eyes narrowed, focusing on him like laser beams, as if she was trying to read his thoughts.

"Why do you do this, Vince?"

"Do what?"

"This. You look after me. Without asking for anything in return."

He swallowed the bite of croissant in his mouth. "We're friends. That's what friends do."

"I don't really know anything about you, do I? I mean, you've never even told me you had a car like that, or you race…I don't even know if you have a girl waiting for you somewhere and, somehow, tonight her man's babysitting me instead. That kind of thing."

He had to smile at her words. She always gave him more credit than he deserved, especially with women. "You know there is no girl. There's no one. As for racing, it's something you don't exactly advertise when you work in a Big Four firm."

"Will you take me to a race next time?"

"I'll take you, just promise you won't tell anyone in the office. With that dress, you'll fit right in."

"This outfit has not been a total waste, then."

"No, not at all." After a quick glance at his watch, he got to his feet. All that talk about his personal life and the absence of romance from it was making him uncomfortable. She would prod and pry all the time, but when she suggested becoming part of it, even in a race, it made him feel exposed, vulnerable. "It's late, Trina. I'd better go."

She nodded and got up, too, following him back to her colorful living room. She handed over his jacket and a paper bag. "The coffee, as promised. If you do decide to bring it to work on Monday, save some for me."

"Not a chance," he said, grinning down at her.

Instead of responding by whacking him on the arm or giving one of her usual silly faces, Trina stared at him with wide, almost doe-like, eyes. She put her arms around his shoulders and invaded what little personal space there was left between them, never taking her gaze off him.

"Trina?" he asked, hesitantly, trapped but not exactly unwilling. "What are you doing?"

"What makes me happy."

With her fingers in his hair, she brought his head down for a kiss.

SEVEN
TRINA

THE HEART

She heard his sharp intake of breath, felt a sudden tautness take over his body. Something fell to the floor, crunching under their feet. The world around them began to spin as she pushed her body against his.

This was something she had never wanted to do with James.

With Vincent, it was the exact opposite. The moment he gave her that big smile, there was nothing more she wanted in the world than to get all that leather off him and have him for herself

She didn't want him to go.

The desire she felt was as clear as the sky on a bright, sunny day. There was neither confusion nor uncertainty. There was only the feeling she was exactly where she was meant to be, with the person she was meant to be with.

His arms, wonderfully warm through her damp clothes, went around her as he started to kiss her back, slowly at first, then with more urgency. He tasted of coffee and rain, of salt and a hint of sugar. She couldn't get enough of it.

In that moment, she realized what she had known, in the deepest and darkest corner of her heart, all along.

It has always been Vincent Tugade.

Kissing alone wouldn't satisfy her. She had never been more certain of something, ever. Her hands took a life of their own, moving beneath his shirt, until she could feel the hardness of his torso under her fingertips.

He didn't keep idle. He nipped at her earlobes and neck as he began to push the straps of the black dress off her shoulders, baring a wider path for his lips to trace.

She moaned when his mouth found its way to her collarbone. She dug her fingers into his back as he devoured the sensitive skin of her throat and chest.

She found her voice and, for what seemed like the very first time, the words to tell him what she truly wanted.

"Please don't go. Don't leave me tonight."

As if wrenched from a dream, he stopped, his hands still on her back, in her hair.

"Trina…" he breathed, his eyes clouding. "I'm sorry."

Her heart was still pounding so loudly in her ears, she could barely hear him. She gripped his shoulders tightly as she fought to catch her breath.

"Sorry? Sorry for what?" She dared herself to look into his eyes.

His silvery gaze seared its way into her soul. She had to look away. She knew she would burn to a bittersweet death if she looked any longer.

"I can't do this, Trina." His voice was subdued, almost melancholic.

"Do what?" Her own response was just as muted.

"I care about you too much to do this now. You deserve so much better than this."

"Vince, please…" She didn't know what she was asking for.

She only knew, at that moment, that she didn't just want him.

She needed him.

He untangled his arms from around her body, but he stayed close enough to cup her face in his hands. "This isn't me rejecting you or us. It's about respecting your feelings and our friendship."

She leaned into his touch. He had to know. Just as she had to go through tonight to find out the truth for herself.

"There's something I need to tell you," she said determinedly, trying to ignore the shakiness and fear in her voice.

He reached for her hand and gave it a reassuring squeeze. "What is it?"

She took a deep breath. "It has always been you."

The words came out in a rush, so she chased after what little bravado she had left. "I never knew how to say it before, because you seemed so unreachable, so... grown-up and perfect."

Vincent didn't say anything, but he stared at her, unblinking, seemingly stunned by the weight of her words.

"Every time I was with someone else, I couldn't help but compare them to you," she continued. "That's why I could never truly be with anyone else—because they would always fall short of what I felt for you. They could never measure up to you, VAT. No one could."

When he finally moved, his reaction was the last thing she expected. He focused on helping her straighten her clothes, his fingers gentle as he smoothed out the creases from her dress like an attentive parent.

When he was done, he pulled her back into his arms for a gentle hug and pressed a soft kiss to her forehead. "Good night, Trina. I'll see you Monday."

Just as he took a step back, her anger flared.

"Good night? That's all you have to say?" She invaded his personal space once more, glaring at him, her raw vulnerability quickly replaced by indignation. "After all we've been through, that's all you've got to say? I don't think you've ever really cared for me, Tugade. All these years, and you never once showed me how much I meant to you!"

In sharp contrast to her biting tone, his response was soft. "That's not true, Trina."

"Isn't it? If you really cared, you would have been smart enough to figure out my feelings for you by now. You would have seen through all my smiles and my teasing, and you would have recognized that it was my love I was trying to hide from you."

"Trina, I..." The words seemed caught in his throat. His face was deathly pale.

He looked a bit like the skull on his jacket, she thought bitterly, stepping away from him and averting her eyes, unable to put up with all the uncertainty surrounding them like a poisonous fog.

"Trina," he began again, more slowly and quietly this time. "I don't just care for you. I love you."

His words landed like a physical blow.

Their meaning was so strong, she was almost thrown backwards onto the floor. Instead, she planted her feet firmly into her damp carpet, stubbornly staring at the wall before her.

Stubbornly refusing to accept what she had just heard.

Vincent didn't stop there. "Maybe that's why you couldn't see it. Caring is something clear, something easily understood. But love..." His voice trailed off, as if he was searching for the right words. "Love is so much more. It's complicated and messy and just plain fucked up. I could never figure out how to show you how I really felt. There's no formula on how to do it."

To her surprise, she felt tears well up in her eyes, taking down the last few pieces that remained of her battered pride. She prayed fervently he couldn't see them—or the pathetic look on her face.

There was a weighted pause before she heard him speak again. "Goodbye, Trina."

She heard a faint rustle as he picked up his jacket from the floor. After a few light footsteps and the creaking of her front door, he was gone.

When she finally had the strength to look, she saw that he'd left the bag of coffee beans behind.

It hurt to move from her spot in the middle of the living room. It was even more excruciating for her to walk to the door and lock it.

She did the only thing she could to ease the pain.

She sat on the couch and gave her tears permission to fall.

EIGHT
VINCENT

THE CHAINS

He felt numb.

He was grateful he could still move after everything that happened in Trina's apartment. His entire body felt frozen and unwilling as he made his way back down the hall and took the elevator. He felt as if he'd run a marathon and then took a beating after.

Vincent climbed into his car and drove away from her building. Through the veil of the ongoing downpour, the streets were nearly empty in the late hour. The deafening roar of his thoughts seemed even more pronounced against the stillness of the world around him.

Why did he leave?

Trina had told him she didn't want him to go. He replayed her words in his mind over and over, each repetition making him question his decision more and more.

"It has always been you."

Wasn't he chained to her all these years? He had always felt that invisible bond connecting them, drawing him closer to her even when he tried to pull away.

"Fuck it all," he muttered under his breath, his hands shaking as he held the steering wheel as tightly as he could, fearing his self-control would slip away at any moment.

Why had he run away now, when she needed him most? Was it fear that held him back? Fear of admitting to himself and to her how much she really meant to him?

He breathed out slowly, trying to calm his racing heartbeat that mirrored the engine's purr.

"Trina," he whispered into the darkness, as if saying her name might bring him a measure of clarity. "I'm sorry, baby. I love you."

As soon as the words left his mouth, he realized that he was making a grave mistake. That the love he had kept bottled up for so long would remain unacknowledged if he didn't turn back.

He couldn't run away now.

He could never run away, in the first place, even if he tried.

Katrina David would always pull at his chains with a single glance, a soft smile, a teasing word; and he would be back right by her side, where he knew he'd always belonged.

Eskeleto's tires screeched on the pavement as he made an abrupt U-turn, his decision made. The streets whirred past him like a kaleidoscope, but all he could focus on was the burning resolve within him.

He accelerated, pushing his car to its limits, just as he would on the track.

But, this time, it was different.

It was a race he didn't want to win. It was a race he desperately wanted to finish.

It was a race he wanted to lose.

Vincent was done running.

I'm coming back for you, Trina.

In no time at all, he was parked outside her apartment building once more. He practically leaped from the car and sprinted to the entrance.

When he arrived at her door, he hesitated for only a second before knocking urgently, not bothering to check if there was a doorbell somewhere on the wall.

Trina opened the door almost immediately.

Her eyes were red and swollen from crying. Her face, which always had the most contagious of smiles, was drawn. She was still wearing her rain-soaked black dress, a little askew around her body after their kisses.

No matter how she looked, she would always be the most beautiful sight to his eyes.

He couldn't hold back any longer.

The words came out in a torrent of emotion. "I'm sorry for running away, Trina. Maybe I wasn't ready to find out how you really felt. It was something I wasn't prepared for...but it's also something I couldn't run away from. And that's why I'm here."

A sob escaped her throat as she flung herself into his arms, her tears warm as they soaked through his shirt. He held her tightly, feeling the weight of years of unspoken feelings finally pouring out between them.

His voice shook when he spoke, but he didn't care. He was done denying his own feelings, too.

"My heart has always belonged to you," he confessed. "In the racing world, they call me the King of Chains, but you have always been my Queen."

"Vincent," Trina whispered against his chest, "for someone so smart, you're an idiot."

He couldn't help but chuckle at her words, knowing the truth behind them. "I promise I won't run anymore, Trina. I'm here. I'll always be here."

"Good," she murmured, pulling back slightly to look into his eyes. "Don't you dare leave me again. And don't even think about leaving me tonight."

As their lips met in a passionate kiss, he knew he would never leave her side ever again.

NINE
TRINA

THE TOUCH

After they kissed each other breathless on her threshold, Vincent spoke against her lips.

"No one is leaving tonight, Trina, as long as you tell me this is what you really want."

She nodded.

He smiled as he gently nudged her into the apartment, shutting the door behind them. Once he had closed them off from the rest of the world, he swept her off the floor and laid her down on the couch, covering her body with his.

Oh, god. She could tell what *he* wanted, felt it through those tight black pants that seemed molded to his long legs, as they resumed their heated kissing. Her own body responded as she shifted her hips closer, higher.

She put her hands on his cheeks and stared into his eyes, unable to stop herself from drowning in them. He was fascinating and so deliciously male. Why did she have to look at other men when she had him in front of her the whole time?

"This is what I've always wanted," she whispered. "I'm very sure."

His lips found hers again. His tongue delved into her mouth as his hands found their way through her clothing. He easily slid the dress off her, followed by her black lace bra and thong.

She had dressed for someone she had never desired, only to be undressed by the one man she had wanted—needed—all this time.

It was worth it, after all, she thought, as she felt him touch that intimate, soaking spot between her legs, felt his mouth close around each of her nipples in turn before making its way down to her heat. She squealed when she felt his tongue on her, her hips bucking wildly. She reached out for him, fumbling with his belt, only to growl and command him to take his clothes off, too.

When he stood bare before her, she marveled at the sheer sight of him. Without clothes, he was more muscle-bound than she'd ever imagined. His tattoos wound around his upper body like chains.

She held out her arms and he went into them. He was very gentle, his voice soft in her ear, promising he would never hurt her. His fingers coaxed her to open, drawing out her pleasure and her need. His lips were on her mouth, on her hair, on her neck, as she ground herself against him, knowing exactly what her body was reaching for.

His timing was exquisite. She felt herself stretch as he entered and sheathed himself inside her. She was the first to move, her hands going up into his hair, her arms locking around his upper back, her teeth grazing his shoulder.

He matched her movements as if they were in a perfectly choreographed dance, his hands on her hips and legs, guiding her body to meet and move against his. He was good, so good.

She felt it then, a warm, snaking sensation beginning to build inside her very core, wrapping itself around her, until she felt it explode between them and send shockwaves of pleasure throughout her body. She heard herself moan his name, followed by incoherent mewls and loud gasps.

"Trina, I love you," he whispered hoarsely, before she felt him tense up and move faster, harder, deeper into her. He made a throaty, guttural sound as his body convulsed on top of hers. She watched pleasure cross his features, savoring how tightly he held on to her, as if for dear life.

She put her arms around him as he slumped on top of her, burying his head between her breasts. She closed her eyes, basking in the bliss that still hummed throughout her body, and the familiar scent and warmth of the man she now had in her arms.

"Vince?" she said into his rumpled hair.

"Yeah?" His eyes were half-closed, his nose nuzzling one breast.

"I'm glad it's you. I've always wanted it to be you."

When she was rewarded by that grin again, and the glitter of what she now recognized as desire in his eyes, she knew they were both in for a long, sleepless night.

In the hours that followed, they explored every corner of her apartment, their bodies coming together in passion and need as they made love over and over again.

From the couch, they rolled down to the living room floor, where he settled her on top of his jacket and put her legs on his shoulders, lifting her hips off the floor as he entered her more deeply than before. She, distantly, heard her loud moans, mixing with his own grunts and groans of pleasure.

With the city lights twinkling through the rain outside the windows, he pressed her against the wall and buried his face between her breasts, their bodies drenched with sweat as they moved and seized pleasure together.

In the kitchen, after they had both eaten more croissants, he devoured her then, using the magic of his tongue, lips and fingers to send her writhing in ecstasy on the tabletop. When he was done, she wrapped her legs around his waist as he took her once more, just as hungrily.

They moved to her bedroom then, where she insisted that she reciprocate what he had done for her in the kitchen. It was then she truly understood how much he really wanted her, and how good he tasted, as he came in her mouth, shouting her name.

In the darkest hours of dawn, their lovemaking became slower, more tender; their earlier desperation and urgency giving way to gentle exploration and intimate confessions.

As the first rays of the sun began to break over the city's skyline, they finally succumbed to exhaustion, collapsing into each other's arms.

As she watched him fall asleep in her embrace, she knew she would never run or hide from him again.

How could she, when her heart had always been his, bound to him with the invisible, unbreakable chains of a love that was there long before she knew it ever existed.

Ten
Vincent

The Light

The first thing he realized, when he woke up, was that he wasn't alone in bed.

Vincent found himself looking at long locks of mahogany hair spread out before him. They belonged to the woman sleeping next to him, spooned naked against his body. He still had one arm around her. Her bare buttocks were pressed against his leg.

He slowly reached over to push the hair away from her face. Trina looked beautifully content in sleep. In the morning light, he could see that her pink lips looked slightly swollen.

Morning light.

There was a small digital clock on the nightstand. It read 9:43.

He had overslept by almost five hours, in a bed that wasn't his.

This bed had sheets and pillowcases in white, orange and pink. A peach-colored teddy bear glared at him from its perch next to the digital clock.

So much for his routine.

But this was the kind of Saturday night and Sunday morning he could get used to.

They had made love all over her apartment, and moved to her bedroom afterwards. After savoring all of her, he decided she tasted like mocha, strong and addictive, with an undeniable hint of sweetness.

The last thing he could recall was Trina grinding on top of him, before he turned her over and took her from behind, tantalized by the perfect roundness of her butt the entire time. At some point, they fell asleep, the rain stopped, and the sun rose, in no particular order.

"Good morning." Her voice was sweet, shy, almost girlish. Her eyes were half-open, still a little clouded with sleep.

"Good morning, baby girl," he said, trying out the endearment for the first time in his life. It sounded right. It felt good to say it.

She turned to face him, her arms going around his neck with surprising familiarity. She kissed him square on the lips. "How'd you sleep?"

"Very good. I just woke up, too. I was watching you."

She blushed and buried her face in his neck. "Don't do that."

"Do what?"

"That thing with your eyes."

He had no idea what she was talking about. "Something wrong with my eyes?"

"No. Yes. Whenever you look at me like that, that's it. I'm gone." Understanding slowly dawned on him, as she began nibbling at his neck.

"Trina?" he prompted, tenderly, reaching for her chin.

"Yes?" She settled against the crook of his arm, as comfortably as she would sit in his office.

"What happens to us now?"

She looked at him with surprise in her eyes but said nothing.

He swallowed. He might as well get it over with, before nerves got the better of him.

"Would you like to be my girlfriend? I suppose, sooner rather than later, I would have to propose, too, seeing that we didn't use—"

She giggled, so merrily he forgot any apprehensions he had. She wriggled closer to him. "To all of the above, my answer is yes."

He kissed her soundly. "I love you."

"I love you, too, although I still can't believe I actually fell in love with someone who's secretly an idiot."

He had to laugh. It was refreshing to have his mental faculties taken down a couple of notches, especially when it came to matters of the heart.

She wasn't finished. "My only condition is that you've got to have the energy for this, Mr. Tugade. I don't want to have fun all by myself."

He raised himself up by the elbow and arranged his demeanor into what she called his Presentation Mode.

"Miss David, allow me to show you the real definition of energy. I hope you're ready for a demonstration."

With her laughter washing over him, he plunged into her waiting arms.

About the Author

Shirley Siaton writes edgy and evocative stories and poems. Her worlds are in a deliciously dark cross-section of the romance, neo-noir, action, fantasy, new adult, and contemporary genres.

She has several books of fiction and poetry released since February 2023. Her first book is the free verse collection *Black Cat and other poems*. She also pens juvenile literature as Shirley Parabia.

She is an award-winning writer, poet, and journalist in English, Filipino and Hiligaynon, lauded by the Stevan Javellana Foundation, Philippine Information Agency, and West Visayas State University. Her essays, short stories, and poems have been published internationally in print and digital media. Her multi-lingual plays have been staged in the Philippines.

Shirley is a black belt in Shotokan Karate and an international certified fitness coach. Originally from Iloilo City, she is based in the Middle East with her husband and two daughters.

On the Web

Shirley's official website:
shirleysiaton.com

Complete reading guide:
shirley.pub

Subscribe to Shirley's VIP list for free exclusive updates:
newsletter.shirleysiaton.com

www.ingramcontent.com/pod-product-compliance
Lightning Source LLC
LaVergne TN
LVHW040108080526
838202LV00045B/3828